# Hotlanta

By Hank Roberts

Edited by Philip Levin

# CHAPTER ONE

From his spot by the elevators, Tom watched the beauty walk into the lobby. Nah, beyond beautiful, she was absolutely gorgeous – a well-assembled 5 foot 4 inches of completely perfect proportions. Her hair was light brown, long and silky, draping over her shoulders like a soft kitten in its mother's arms. She wore a skimpy mini skirt with a leather jacket, sky-blue silk blouse, and stylish but practical flat shoes. She captured the gaze of every man in the hotel lobby as she made her way to the sign-in desk pulling her small suitcase.

He put away his cell phone and wandered closer. When she glanced his way, he pretended to be interested in the potted plant next to him. Glancing back, he got a good look at her face. The eyes on this model were coffee colored, with some golden flecks sprinkled in. Her lips were soft and tender like divinity candy. Tom listened as the clerk confirmed her name, address, and payment method, and then handed her the room key.

"Help with your luggage, ma'am?" the bellboy asked.

She nodded, handing him a five-dollar bill. "Please take it on up to my room. I've got to rush out for a meeting."

She strode into the elevator and Tom watched the numbers indicate she'd taken it down to the second level underground parking garage. He hurried down the steps and opening the door quietly, spotting her about forty yards ahead.

He was about to follow closer when a thuggish appearing man in jeans and a pullover sweatshirt stepped out from behind a pole.

"Hey, Honey. What's your hurry?" he said with a sneer.

Tom stepped out of the stairwell and shouted. "Hey, you!"

The man turned towards Tom, giving the woman the chance to go on the attack. With three quick moves, she disabled the attacker and had him lying on his stomach with his arms behind his back. Reaching behind and under her leather jacket, she pulled out a set of handcuffs, popping them on his wrists.

"Hey copper," she called turning towards Tom.

Tom stood with arms on hips just a few steps into the garage. "Are you talking to me?"

"I'm not talking to the jerk and there isn't anyone else in this garage. Come over here."

Tom strolled up to her, looking down at the bad guy trundled up. "You did a good job, little lady. Of course, I helped by distracting him. In another few seconds I'd have come to your rescue."

She snorted. "Oh, of course you would have, like some sort of knight in shining armor, huh? You are a cop, aren't you?"

Tom raised an eyebrow. "What makes you say that?"

The way you scoped me out in the lobby. At first, I figured you for a pervert but then gave you the benefit of the doubt. Cop, right?"

"One of the best you'll ever meet. I'm Tom Hill, assistant chief of police here in Atlanta.

Welcome to our fine city, by the way, Miss …. Miss …?" He held out a hand.

She looked at the roof with an OMG expression and ignored his handshake offer. "Well, Chief Hill, here's a perp I've captured for you. Deal with him any way you'd like. I've got a meeting to go to." She turned and strode off.

"Hey, what's your name?" he called after her. "I can't charge him without you filing a complaint."

She popped into her red Triumph convertible and slammed its door behind her. She backed up, pulling next to Tom and pausing. "Then let him go. I don't care what you do." She burnt rubber as she sped up the ramp and away.

Tom unhooked the handcuffs and released the bum, shooing him off with a warning. Returning to the hotel check-in desk, he recorded the woman's name and hometown, Ester Allison, D.C., in his notebook. He considered the way she'd taken down that thug and that she lived in the capital.

"Must be a government agent," he figured.

Though now a police executive, he still liked walking the streets whenever he could. It gave him opportunities to meet the people, the poor and the rich, the good and the misguided. A lot were local, but then again, a lot of strangers came into town. He had to admit he burned with curiosity about this gorgeous government karate specialist.

# CHAPTER TWO

Tom answered his cell phone to find Alice, one of his two secretaries, on the line. "The mayor wants to see you right away," she told him. "He's at The Capital Grille. Says there's someone there you've already met but need to be introduced to."

"What does that mean?" Tom shot back, but Alice didn't know, so he hung up and went out to his car. The drive from the hotel through midday Atlanta traffic took him nearly twenty-minutes. As soon as he got out of his car, he was escorted into a back-dining room whose entrance was guarded by four uniformed policemen.

Inside, he found three men and a woman. He already knew two of the men. Daniel Stife, the gray-haired chief of police, his boss and good friend, stepped forward to shake Tom's hand and introduce him. Pot-bellied Mayor Whitely he also already knew. He shared greetings with the next fellow, a tall muscular man introduced as Stan Hamburg, DEA agent in charge of the Atlanta region. The last dinner guest was indeed someone he'd met but hadn't been introduced to. It was Ester, the woman from the hotel.

He offered his hand with a smirk, and this time she took it. "See," he said. "It pays to have manners."

She snorted. "As no doubt you found out by snooping at the hotel, my name is Ester Allison. I'm the FBI agent assigned to this project. Let's set two things straight at the beginning. We're going to work together, so let's treat each other with dignity and respect."

Tom held up his hands in mock defensiveness. "As I remember, it was you who refused the handshake. What's the second thing?"

"I'm in charge, not you."

The four sat at the table in the private room, waiting until the waitstaff had served the food before starting the meeting. Once the door was closed behind them, Hamburg stood up.

"Thank you all for your time. I suppose everyone here but Mr. Hill knows what's up?"

Mayor Whitley answered. "I don't know anything more than what Daniel told me this morning. Something about illegal drugs?"

"That's right," Hamburg confirmed. "The DEA has discovered that Atlanta has become the hub of drug trafficking for a large cartel out of Colombia. Somehow, they're getting in huge quantities of heroin undetected on a regular basis. In order to shut it down, we need to locate the drop off mechanism and arrest the middlemen. FBI agent Allison, here, will be in charge of this operation. We want to keep this on a strict need-to-know basis. She's expecting the full cooperation of the local police department."

Daniel turned to his friend. "That's why you're here, Tom. I'm putting you in charge of this operation from a local standpoint. You're to create a task force of six. Actually, I've already talked to one, your friend Manuel Gomez. As I'm sure you know, he's a Colombian native."

After the meeting, Tom made personal visits to each of the city's precinct chiefs. A seventy-four-degree spring day, he drove with windows open, enjoyed traveling around the city *en route* to visiting all the different spots around town. In his discussions, he didn't give any details, just asked them to relay the message to their officers to report anything having to do with heroin.

Throughout the day, Tom received 127 reports from the city precincts. He tried to follow up each one, but the papers piled up faster than he could deal with them. By five o'clock he'd only worked through thirty-six of the reports. Tense and weary, he barked his hello into the phone when it rang.

"I called to ask how you're holding up," Ester said, "but the sound of your voice tells me not so well."

Tom crumpled the latest report into a hard-little ball in his fist. "I'm doing just fine, Agent Allison. I'm no puss."

"Really? And because I'm a female, that makes me a puss, right? Not finding it so easy doing deskwork? I guess you consider that the kind of job for women, right? They tell me you're the kind of officer who'd rather be out on the streets."

"Yeah, that's right. I'm a cop for the people. I love being out meeting the citizens. You know, I got cop-of-the-year twice."

"I'm SO impressed," she said, her voice dripping with sarcasm. "Listen, Hill. You look sharp: tall, handsome, and well dressed. But pomp isn't going to impress these guys. Colombian drug dealers would just as soon shoot you down as spit on you. Maybe it's a good time for you to be inside after all."

Chief Tom stared at the phone, his mouth curled in a sneer. "We'll see who can take care of themselves when the shit hits the fan," he replied, slamming down the receiver.

"I hope I can with her," he murmured. "She may be beautiful, but that's not all that it takes to be classy." With a sigh, he returned to the papers piled in front of him. He had them organized in neat stacks, each color-coded and identified by a tag with the number of the precinct it came from.

The door opened and Chief Daniel Snife, came in. "I've got a confirmed rumor that the next big shipment of heroin is going to come by plane early next week. What do you think?"

Tom sat back in his chair, a pencil against his forehead as he thought. "Two possibilities. It could come into the main airport. That's certainly been done before. Usually there're several inside agents. Do we have anyone working on that?"

"Yeah," Daniel told him. "The FBI is all over that angle. What else?"

"Heroin's big, but it isn't huge. A private jet could be flying to a small local airport, unloading, and then returning to Colombia. I'll put together a list of private fields that seem likely targets and send my task force out to each one."

"How's your task force coming?"

Tom pulled out his notebook and read off five names, including Manuel Gomez. "I've known all these guys for at least five years. They're good cops."

"And the sixth?'

Tom shook his head. "That cow of an FBI agent, Allison, says she'll be the sixth … and in charge."

Daniel gave him a wink. "You kind of like her, don't you?"

Tom's mouth dropped. "LIKE her? Hell. Don't get me started."

Daniel laughed, and then turned serious. "What about an inside man?"

"I was wondering that. I presume you assigned me Manuel for that purpose, but I'm not so sure. It would be terribly dangerous. Manuel's just been married a year and his wife just delivered their first child. I'd hate to send him down there and have something happen to him."

Daniel put a hand on Tom's shoulders. "This job isn't easy, my friend. Sometimes you have to send a friend into danger. But it's our job."

After the chief had left, Tom called Manuel Gomez in. Since he grew up in Columbia, Manuel was fluent in both the country's language and its customs.

"How's that new baby of yours?" Tom asked.

Manuel grinned. "Came in at nine pounds. He's going to be an athlete someday."

"Like his dad," Tom replied, referring to Manuel's short but muscular build. He indicated for Manuel to take the seat opposite him.

"There's a situation. I want to make it clear that you can turn this assignment down. It might be dangerous."

He waited for Manuel to nod his understanding before continuing.

"I'm in charge of a task force that's going to shut down a drug cartel shipping heroin from Colombia to Atlanta. We think they're using small planes and a regional airport. Chief Snife suggested we might benefit from an inside man. It would mean going into Colombia as an undercover agent. What do you think?"

Manuel sat back in his chair and twilled his well combed mustache. "When do you want me to leave?"

"Say the day after tomorrow? It'll give both of us a chance to make proper preparations."

Over the next 48 hours, Tom booked Manuel on a flight and into a local hotel. Tom managed to get Manuel a job to start work on Monday at the main Bogota shipping service out at the airport. He handed him an international satellite cell phone and told him to leave a message each morning on his desk recorder. Tom would only contact him back if Manuel asked.

The trip went without incident. Manuel spent the first couple of days getting the feel of the city and the local politics. On Monday he showed up for the job at 8 a.m., and soon was hard at work, pushing around luggage and dealing with shipping issues. He got along well with his co-workers, just one-of-the-guys, and after the first day's work, he joined them for beer at the local bar.

On his third night, around a card game, he heard one of his coworkers discuss a big shipment that had been flown out the night before to a private airport near Atlanta. Being careful not to arouse suspicion, Manuel was able to find out that these kinds of shipments went out about once a week, headed to a small airport just northwest of Atlanta.

When Tom got this information from Manuel's recorded message the next day, he made a list of all the airstrips in the region, then based on factors such as population density, police presence, and security, narrowed the choices down to three.

He called Ester. "Okay, Agent Allison. My source came through, like, I knew he would. I inspire great men, Allison. Here's the list of the three most likely airports." He read them off to her.

"Got it," she confirmed.

"He says a shipment went out last night. If you hurry, you might even catch them red-handed."

# CHAPTER THREE

Ester had checked out the first two airports on Tom's list and quickly ruled them out. Now, at the third one, a small field surrounded by woods in a semi-rural, hilly suburb of the city, she had the feeling she'd found the right spot. Surrounded by forest on all sides but the road, it would be relatively easy for a small plane from Colombia to land in the middle of the night. No one would notice, and they'd be able to get the shipment of heroin out by the highway.

Beginning on their arrival at noon, Ester and the four Atlanta officers Tom had assigned her had spent the afternoon hours surveying every square foot of the facility known as Aire Bueno Aeroport. It was a relatively small private airport, twenty hangers, an office building, two parking lots, one for planes and one for cars, and, of course, a runway. A couple of outbuildings also sat against the fenced perimeter. Flood lights were arranged along the approach area to make it possible to use the airfield at night.

On the far right, toward the fence yet close to the tarmac, sat an old DC-9 airplane that the fire department apparently had been using for firefighting practice. Its wings were collapsed onto the ground and the entire exterior of the plane had been severely scorched.

They searched every square inch of the airport, both inside and out, even bringing drug dogs, who sniffed all the buildings. In the late afternoon Tom showed up to check on their progress.

"Any luck?" he asked.

Ester glared at him. "Not a sign of any drugs. I'm beginning to wonder if you purposely sent me on a wild goose chase."

"Not intentionally. You interview anyone?"

"The whole day only three people have come and gone. There were two fellows who came to fly their plane to Chicago and another pilot who just came in to check on his plane. We vetted them and clearly they had nothing to do with the drugs."

"What about the office fellow?"

"Bubba Simpson? He's seventy-six years old, half deaf and half stupid. He's just here to make fresh coffee for the pilots and make sure raccoons don't get into the hangers and damage the planes. There's also a cleaning service and a security drive-through service. We'll have to check those out later."

Tom took out his notebook and looked at the list of three airports. "You're sure it's not one of the other two?"

"No. But just because we didn't find anything today, doesn't rule this place out completely. For now, though, we're done. Be sure and let me know as soon as you hear anything more from your agent."

One of the Atlanta officers came up to Tom and asked if they were done for the day and could go home.

He pointed over his shoulder at Ester. "She claims to be the boss. Ask her."

Tom walked away towards the DC-9. He loved old planes. As a kid he used to build models of them. Reaching the machine, he stroked the wing, and then headed to the cockpit.

Just before stepping into the plane, a shot rang out, and he grimaced as a bullet went through the muscles of his right shoulder. He lost his balance on the cockpit steps and tumbled to the dirt below. The officers all jumped out of their cars, guns pulled out, but no one could tell where the shot had come from. With so much woods surrounding the airport, the shot could have come from anywhere.

Ester ran over to examine the extent of Tom's injury. As she leaned down close to his shoulder to check the wound, her long silky hair draped over his body. The smell of her perfume made Tom smile.

"Now that's the way that I think you ought to approach your fellow officer," he said. "I'll remember this sight forever."

"Mind your manners, Officer Hill. We need to call for backup and an ambulance."

Tom sat up and shook his head. "Nah. The shooter's obviously gone or he'd still be firing at us. My wound's minor. I'll just bandage it up at home."

Ester snorted. "You think you're Mister Macho, Officer Hill, but I know regulations. You're sitting right here until the ambulance arrives and get this wound properly evaluated. While you're there, I hope they do some psychological examinations on you as well."

While they were waiting for the ambulance, Ester commented that they must have been close to something, otherwise, why would someone take a shot at him?

"We searched this old plane thoroughly," she added.

"Maybe they land, unload into another vehicle, and then take off again," Tom suggested.

"That's possible, though in general that increases the risk, especially if they're doing it at night. In our experience, it's more common to unload the drugs and have them picked up later. It lowers the number of people exposed to being caught, as well as decreasing attention."

The next morning, on the way to the hospital to visit Tom, Ester considered her impressions of him. He was handsome and dressed sharply.

Although rude to her, he generally seemed to have decent manners. He hadn't whined after being shot, and she liked her men tough.

As she entered Tom's hospital room, she saw two lovely ladies kissing him on the cheeks. Ester noticed the women wore wedding rings.

"Looks like I have serious competition," Ester observed.

The women stepped over and offered their hands, which Ester shook. They introduced themselves as Alice and Mary, Tom's secretaries.

"So you're the FBI agent Tom was telling us about," Alice said. "You are as good looking as he said." The two women giggled.

"ALICE!" Tom shouted.

"Tom told us you're from D.C. and you pack quite a punch," Mary added. "Will you be staying long?"

"I'm not sure. I'm on assignment for a special project."

Alice and Mary glanced at each other, and then Alice said, "How about we pick you up at your hotel Wednesday night and take you out for dinner, drinks, and a bit of girl talk?"

Ester gave her a big smile. "That'd be wonderful. I don't have any friends here, of course. I'm staying at the Marriot Marquis. Here's my card."

"We've got to get back to the office," Mary reported. Turning to Tom, she said, "We'll tell them at the office you survived your major surgery. Meanwhile, you rest and follow the doctor's orders." The two secretaries gave Ester the traditional Southern good-bye hug and left.

"They seem nice enough," Ester said.

"Yeah, and they're excellent secretaries," Tom confirmed. "Both are happily married, by the way. Here, they've brought me a box of chocolate. Would you like a piece?" Tom extended the box to Ester, who chose the chocolate-covered cherry.

"How sure are you about the information you got from Bogota?" she asked.

"Manuel's very reliable, but, well, undercover work is always difficult. You have to work with rumors. Let's review all you found at the site."

Ester took out her notebook and showed Tom the sketches she'd made of the airport. "We didn't find anything suspicious, and the dogs didn't sniff any drugs. Looks like a dead-end."

"Then why did someone shoot me?"

She shook her head. "Could have nothing to do with the drugs. Some people just don't like cops."

Tom examined the drawings she had handed him. "It's mostly tarmac which won't show any tracks."

"Right. The only tracks were those left by the fire trucks near the beat-up DC-9. Other than that, there was nothing."

"I'm curious about these flood lights," Tom said, pointing to them on the drawing. "How do they work?"

"The planes have a frequency signal they can send out that turns them on and off at night. Unless the pilots turn them off, they're set to go off automatically after half an hour."

Tom sighed. "What are we going to tell Mayor Whitley? He's going to be disappointed that this hasn't panned out."

"Don't be discouraged. We know the shipments are coming in weekly so there's still plenty of more chances to find the transport plane. Why don't we see if we can get information on all flights in and out of Colombia and maybe we'll be ready for the next one."

"Good idea. I'll call my contacts at the airport traffic control for a list of all flights that have arrived from Columbia over the past month, especially any landing at the smaller airports."

# CHAPTER FOUR

One evening, a few days into Manuel's work at the airport, he met up at a local bar with a half-dozen of his new friends. Most were quite poor, like himself, living off of airport wages that barely provided for the basic needs. However, he noticed that two of the men had expensive clothes, shiny shoes, pressed slacks, and gold jewelry. He went up to one.

"How's it going, Pedro?" he asked. "Buy you a drink?"

Pedro looked Manuel over, observing his worn out and grease stained clothing. "How about I treat you to one instead?" He pulled out a crisp American hundred-dollar bill and called to the bartender.

"Here, Jesus. Put everyone's drinks on my tab."

A cheer went up from the group and everyone ordered their favorite drink. Pedro took Manuel off to a private corner booth.

"You're new here, aren't you?" Pedro asked.

"I'm from Tunja originally," Manuel replied. "I've been living in the United States for the past five years, but the immigration people found me and shipped me back. Got a job here to send money to my old mother back home. She's got diabetes and can't get around, you know. Sure is tougher living on Colombian wages than it was with the salary I was earning in the States."

Pedro nodded, and the two drank in silence for a couple of minutes. Around them the sounds of the bar grew louder, an accordion song blasting its rhythm from tinny speakers and around the pool table a few of the men were arguing. A prostitute came up to their table, but Pedro shooed her away.

"You speak English, then?" Pedro asked.

"Well, I'd never pass as a native, but I can speak and understand it well. Why?"

For another few minutes they drank in silence. "I'm wondering if you'd be interested in making some extra money, you know, for your poor mother."

Manuel took one of the jalapeños from the bowl on the table and took a big bite, washing it down with a beer. He looked around the room again, making sure no one was paying them any attention.

"Yeah, I might be interested. What do you have in mind?"

"I've got a friend who hires extra people for special shipments. It's all hush hush, but pays pretty well. There's one coming up Tuesday night. If you're interested, I could let the boss know."

"I guess so. How much money and how much work?"

"You keep your mouth shut and it'll get you five-hundred bucks U.S. for just three hours work. Gotta be done in the middle of the night, though. You in?"

Manuel gave a low whistle. "Five-hundred dollars? That'd get my mama a new wheelchair. You bet! Thanks, Pedro. You can count on me."

Before going to work the next morning, Manuel called Tom and left the message about the next shipment being loaded on Tuesday.

On Tuesday evening at ten p.m., Manuel reported to the designated location, where, with three other men, he transferred fifty waterproof wrapped packages from a truck into the luggage area of a small Cessna. He memorized the plane's call numbers. Within two hours all of the work had been done. When he got home, he discovered an envelope sitting on his cabinet. Inside, he found five crisp one-hundred-dollar bills. He put them under his pillow and went to sleep.

Ester, Tom, and their team had arrived at the airport by late-afternoon, Tuesday. Bubba, the maintenance man, was told to leave and lock the gates, hanging a closed sign on it. They posted two sharpshooters on the office building's roof, the three other officers at various points around the hangers. Ester and Tom waited inside the office which had only a single light over the coffee machine.

"You think they're coming?" Ester asked.

"Stakeouts can be boring and you gotta hang tough. I once stayed at a stakeout for seventy-hours straight before I was able to grab my suspect. If this is too much for you, head back to your hotel and I'll call you in the morning."

Ester glared at him. "Listen, buster. I'm tired of hearing your boasts and having you put me down. You saw what I did to that perp at the hotel. You want some of that, you just keep up with your braggadocios ways."

Just after 2:15 in the morning, they heard a plane approaching. The flood lights switched on and a Cessna landed and taxied on the tarmac towards the row of private hangers. Suddenly, all the floodlights went dark. Ester looked over at Tom who shrugged.

"Maybe there's an electrical issue. Let's see what happens."

After fifteen minutes, the lights came back on. Apparently, the plane hadn't moved in all that time, but with the lights back on, it resumed its approach, pulling into one of the hangers and shutting down its engines. The three ground officers and Tom and Ester surrounded the plane, their guns at the ready.

Four passengers came out, hands up, looking bewildered. They were well dressed, the three men in suits and the woman in a business outfit.

"What's going on?" one asked.

"FBI," Ester said, showing her badge. Please stand over by the wall, keeping your hands up." She pointed to the pilot who'd remained in his seat. "You too." When he didn't move, she repeated the command in Spanish, and he climbed out of the plane and joined the passengers under guard by one of the officers.

Tom and Ester and another officer searched the plane, realizing quickly that there were no drugs on board.

Ester went to the passengers and demanded their papers.

"Mr. Stephen Gonzalez? It says here you're an American citizen," she said.

"Of course," the man replied, with only a slight Spanish accent. "I own a jewelry business in Atlanta and was down in Colombia buying some gold pieces to sell at my store. This is my wife and two of my salesmen. Everything's perfectly legitimate. We filed the appropriate papers with the FAA and customs and immigration. What's with all this fuss?"

She handed Mr. Gonzalez his papers. "I apologize for your inconvenience. We run spot checks from time to time on planes coming from foreign countries. I'm sure you understand."

Mr. Gonzalez looked at the half dozen officers. "Really? All these people for a spot check?"

She gave him a smile. "Yes, routine." She then spoke to the pilot in Spanish. Turning to Tom she reported, "The pilot wants to know if he can refuel and head back to Colombia tonight."

Tom looked around the hanger. "Looks like there's no reason to keep him I guess."

The next morning Tom listened to Manuel's message. He reported that he had helped load fifty well-wrapped packages into the small plane. He provided the call numbers for the Cessna, and hoped the bust went well.

Tom confirmed the plane's call numbers with the ones Manuel had given him. They matched.

An hour later, Chief Snife came in.

"What went wrong?" he asked.

"Don't know yet, but I promise I'll find out. Manuel's message this morning confirmed that this was the right plane and that he had helped load it with drugs. I'm waiting on the written reports from all the officers that were there. Maybe one of the sharpshooters on the roof saw something. I already sent two investigators out there first thing this morning, telling them to search the small outer buildings and the old DC-9 again."

Two hours later Tom got a call from one of the investigators.

"Anything new?" Tom asked.

"No trace of drugs. But there is one interesting item. There are new tire tracks leading to the old DC-9 that weren't there when I was out here Saturday. I'm out here at fire station number twelve. Tracks match the treads on one of their two engines."

"Did you ask them?"

"Yeah, of course, I'm here now. There are four guys on duty, and one of them told me that a couple of firemen took the truck out to the airport

Sunday for a practice, but those two aren't on duty right now."

"Sunday, but not last night?"

Tom could hear the officer's voice as he asked one of the firemen about the previous night. A mumble came back.

"They say no one stays at this small unit at night. If there's a fire, there's a list of on-call firemen who live close enough that they can get to the station within ten minutes to respond. Someone could have taken the truck out last night they suppose, but as far as they know, no one did."

Tom hung up the phone, thoughts racing through his brain. "All rats leave a trail, even if it's very slight. With the right dog to sniff them out, all trails can be uncovered."

That evening Tom was relaxing on his couch with a nice cold beer when his phone rang.

"Are you available for dinner tonight?" Ester asked. "Let's meet at McGill's and discuss the case. It's close to your house, right?"

Tom frowned. McGill's was one of his favorite restaurants, partly because it was only two blocks from his townhouse.

"Yeah, I'll come. Let's see, it's quarter of seven now. How about I meet you there at 7:36?"

"7:36? What a strange time to set. Why not 7:30?"

Tom replied, "I don't like meeting at even half hour times because it makes me too predictable. Speaking of which, is it just going to be the two of us? Does anyone else know of our clandestine meeting?"

Ester laughed. "Don't be so paranoid. It's just a business meeting."

At 7:36 exactly, Tom arrived at the restaurant, finding Ester waiting at the bar. "You don't have any friends around with guns, do you?" he asked.

"No. If my friends had shot at you, we'd have taken you to the morgue, not the hospital. Here, I got us both a beer. It's your favorite brand."

He looked at it and back at her. "How did you know that this was my brand ... and how did you know McGill's was close to my apartment?"

She gave him a wink. "It's my job to know things."

Tom took his drink and helped Ester off her stool, noticing her long shapely legs peeking out from under her dress. He followed her to a table.

He ordered a burger, and Ester a vegetarian lasagna. When it arrived, she shook salt onto her dish several times.

"I noticed you salted your food before tasting it," he said. According to standard personality profiles, that predicts that you're impetuous and likely to act on instinct instead of waiting for facts."

She snickered. "Or it might mean that I've eaten at this restaurant before and know that they don't salt their lasagna enough."

As they ate, Ester asked him about the reliability of his officer in Colombia.

"I've known Manuel for five years and always found him trustworthy. You know, he's risking his life down there, trying to infiltrate the drug ring. He said he loaded packages into the plane, and I believe him. What happened after that is what we need to figure out."

Ester asked, "If he loaded a shipment of something onto that plane, how did they get rid of it?"

"I don't know. He says they were well packaged. If they still had the shipment when the plane landed, they might have somehow gotten rid of it in the fifteen minutes that the lights went out. Yet those four passengers clearly hadn't done any labor. They looked like they'd been relaxing in the plane's comfortable seats for four hours without a care in the world. Have you ever had a case like this before?"

Ester took the last bite of her meal. "Good," she said. "Needed more salt." She pushed her plate away. "Yes, I've had several drug cases over the last couple of years, some with very interesting twists." She began telling of her cases, and Tom reciprocated. Before they knew it, it was eleven p.m. and the restaurant was closing."

"How are you feeling?" Tom asked.

"What do you mean?"

"Well, we've both had a lot to drink, and we're having enjoyable conversation. How about we take an evening walk? As you know, it's only two blocks to my place. We can have another beer and continue our conversation."

Ester cocked her head. "You're inviting me to come to your townhouse for the night?"

Tom held up his palms. "I'm a gentleman, there's no implications here. I have a nice couch where you can crash."

Her frown turned into a bit of a wry smile. "Well, it is a nice evening for a walk. Okay, then."

Tom tried to pick up the tab, but Ester insisted they go Dutch. In the cool evening air, they continued talking about their work, and soon reached his home.

# CHAPTER FIVE

Just inside the door, Tom took off his shoes, placing them on the shelf he kept there for the purpose. He indicated for Ester to do the same, enjoyed the view of her long legs peeking out from her skirt as she lifted each one to remove its shoe. He went to the refrigerator and brought out two beers, opened them, and handed one to Ester. They settled at his kitchen table.

She looked around his living room, noting his very tidy bookshelves with each row exactly aligned by size and color. He'd decorated in beige earth tones, with a soft leather couch and deep armchairs. The walls held a series of framed Dick Tracy comic-book covers, perfectly hung.

She took out her notepad with the map of the airport.

"Look, our sources say that the heroin is coming into Atlanta. That means the plane didn't drop it off on the way and must have landed with it. That means the only time they could have unloaded the heroin was that time of darkness when the plane was on the tarmac. I'm suspicious of the DC-9. Afterall, that's where you got shot."

Tom took a sip of his beer, setting it back carefully on its napkin. "Yet you searched the entire area, especially the two small storage buildings and the old DC-9 wreck. No trace of drugs or recent activity."

Ester yawned. "Well I'm bushed. How about we get some sleep and we'll talk about it more in the morning."

"Sure." He stood up. "Wait here and I'll be right back with some sheets for the couch and a fresh towel. You can have the bathroom first."

In the middle of the night, Tom snapped awake. He had heard his door click. Squinting in the dim lighting, he saw a shadow entering his room. He eased his pistol out from under his pillow, sat up and snapped on the light.

Ester looked at him wide-eyed.

"Don't shoot! I had to go pee again."

Tom grinned, putting the gun back under his pillow. "Sorry, I'd forgotten for a moment you were here." He noticed that she had stripped down to a camisole and panties and boy did she look hot! He kept the light on until she was done and back in the living room. As he turned off his lamp, he thought, "Some memories will last forever … or at least I hope so."

The next morning Tom awoke to the smell of bacon and eggs being fried by Ester. He showered and shaved, dressing in fresh clothing, everything neatly put together. When he came into the kitchen, he saw that Ester had commandeered one of his flannel shirts as her only clothing. He tried hard not to stare at her gorgeous gams showing below.

After breakfast she put on her clothes from the previous night. He dropped her off at her car and watched as she drove off in the cute little convertible.

"Man, that's one hot officer," he mused, as he made his way to work. "Too bad we're working together and can't get more personal."

When Tom arrived at his office, he noticed that both Alice and Mary wore huge smiles. "Y'all look like a mule eating briars," he said. "What's up?"

Both ladies settled back in their chairs and tried to look busy. But then they started giggling.

"Damn it, what's up?" Tom demanded.

Alice looked at him. "Last night we had plans to go out with Ester, but when we got to her hotel, she was already gone. We drove around a bit and spotted her car at McGill's. That little sporty Triumph is pretty easy to spot, you know. We thought we'd join her there, but when we went in, we saw the two of you having a private *tête-à-tête*, and figured we'd best leave you alone. This morning I drove past McGill's and saw her car was still there."

"What we want to know," Mary said, "is whether she's as cute undressed as she is dressed?"

Tom glared at them. "First, we were having a business dinner discussing the investigation. Second, my personal life is none of your business."

Once in his office he went over the notes his officers had made. No one had found anything unusual at the airport, neither during the landing of the plane nor on the many inspections they'd made since. Manuel's daily report was routine.

Tom and Ester felt confident that the next time the shipment came, they'd be ready. It was just a matter of waiting, so Tom and Ester had a little free time to enjoy each other. Tom took her to some of Atlanta's landmarks, including the aquarium and a Braves' game, and to his surprise he found that they shared common interests in everything. Tom realized he really liked Ester but wasn't sure if he wanted to get romantic with her. He knew sleeping with a work buddy could lead to big trouble.

Monday morning, Manuel's recorded message made him excited. "We're loading the next shipment tomorrow night. Oh, and one other thing. I've noticed that every time the DC-9 is mentioned Pedro laughs."

"There's GOT to be something about that plane," Tom insisted to Ester.

"Okay, then, let's go check it out again."

She drove Tom out to the airport in her sports car, zipping between lanes and darting into gaps barely wide enough. Once they hit the outskirts with its winding country roads, she turned into a speed demon, whizzing around trucks with little regard to oncoming traffic, and on straightaways, reaching ninety mph.

"SLOW DOWN!" Tom shouted against the wind rushing through the car.

She glanced at him and laughed. "Mussing up your hair?"

After she parked next to the DC-9, she hopped right out, but he held onto the car door for a good fifteen seconds before trying to walk to the plane.

"There's got to be something here," she insisted, when he joined her inside.

He looked around the cockpit, his brow furrowed. "There's something wrong here."

"What?"

"Well, I used to study airplanes when I was younger, been in several ones like this. These seats aren't standard."

"You sure? I mean, they're pretty burnt up from all the fires they've been through."

Tom brushed the ashes off one of the seats. "Look, there's some sort of trap door hidden here." He pulled it open and revealed a large well protected cavity. The two officers stared at each other.

"This is it!" he shouted. "They stop on the runway and unload the drugs into the containers on this plane."

Ester had a huge smile. "I bet you're right. Then someone from the fire department retrieves the packages and takes them out to distribute to the dealers. Case solved! When that plane lands in the early morning hours tomorrow tonight we can make our bust."

The next night, Tuesday, the seven-member task force were again staked out at the airport. At 3:30 Wednesday morning the plane landed, and, just like before, all the lights in the airport went out as they were parked on the runway. However, this time the Atlanta police were prepared. They'd parked their cars facing the runway and when the airport lights went out, they all turned on their headlights, jumped out of their cars, and rushed the plane, flashlights and guns in hand. They heard some type of loud clang.

There were three gentlemen as passengers, as well as a pilot, this one different than the one from the previous week. All were escorted off to huddle in a small group on the tarmac. Walking around the plane, the officers found that the luggage door in the back was hanging open, and inside they found that area stuffed full of well-packaged heroin.

Tom picked up one package and carried it to where the group was standing. "You want to confess now, or wait until we get to the police station?"

"I'm very sorry, Señor," one of the men said. "We have no idea what you are talking about."

"Don't act dumb," Tom growled. "Your plane is stuffed with heroin."

"Heroin?!" The men turned to each other, apparently in astonishment. "No, no, Señor," the man insisted. "There must be some mistake. We're civil engineers coming up for a conference. We chartered this plane last week. We know nothing about heroin."

Tom guffawed. "Right. Tell it to the judge."

The men and the pilot were arrested and three of the officers were sent back to the city with the prisoners. The other two were stationed at the airport to watch for the fire engine, and arrest whoever was driving it when they showed up. Ester and Tom both went back to their respective places with a feeling that they'd accomplished their mission.

# CHAPTER SIX

Having gotten home at five in the morning, Tom didn't get back to the office until one. There he was greeted with cheers and congratulatory messages from dozens of officers, including a special thank-you from the mayor's office. Alice and Mary both kissed him on the cheek.

Once settled in, Tom had time to listen to Manuel's daily message.

"There's a lot of buzz, but I'm not sure what happened. Did you bust the cartel? Can I come home? In any case, I've been invited to a meeting at the boss's home tonight. Only the people that he really likes gets to come to his home. I think they like me because I'm a hard worker and I know how to keep my mouth shut. I hope that I can get some pertinent information while I'm there. His name is Don Carlos Cantrell, and he owns a big hacienda just outside of Bogota. I'll report again tomorrow about tonight's dinner."

Tom sent two of his team to relieve the two who'd kept vigil at the airport. They reported no one had shown up.

"I guess someone warned the contact at the fire department that the shipment was disrupted," Tom said. "We'd better go down there and check it out."

This time Tom insisted on being the driver. On the way he said, "You've got to admit, me and my men did a damn good job busting this operation in a matter of two weeks. Turns out we didn't need your FBI expertise after all."

Ester didn't answer, just stared out the window.

"What? You're not going to congratulate me? You can head back to your little life in D.C. now that I've solved your problem."

She shook her head. "There're things that don't make sense here."

"What?"

"Both times the passengers seemed to be perfectly legitimate travelers that knew nothing about the heroin. Even if they were lying, neither group seemed capable of transferring that much heroin from the cargo bay into the plane in fifteen minutes."

"Maybe they're well trained?"

"Don't forget all the ashes on that plane. Our hands and clothes were both filthy after yesterday's quick exam. Those first passengers were spotless, both in their clothes and their hands."

Tom considered her words. "You have a point. Still, we caught them red-handed with the heroin. You have any other idea how that heroin could have been unloaded?"

"No." They drove in silence for a bit longer before she asked, "What did the pilot say?"

"I haven't gotten the transcribed interview," Tom admitted. "But the interviewer told me he's just a commercial licensed pilot who flies planes on medium size jaunts like this several times a week. He claims to know nothing of the heroin. He just followed instructions to land, turn off the lights for fifteen minutes, and then turn them back on."

"He didn't think that was strange?"

Tom shrugged. "Apparently, he was getting paid to do something and he did it."

In another few minutes she said, "There's another thing bothering me."

"Yeah? What other crazy problem has gotten into that little bitty female brain of yours?"

She ignored the insult, having gotten used to his innuendos. "Remember how much room that heroin took up in the plane? It seems to me there wasn't enough room in those DC-9 seats to hold all of that."

At the fire station they met Bill Melton, the local fire chief. After examining their credentials, he invited them to join him in his small office. It had a musty, crowded feel. Pictures of shapely women wearing little clothing and holding big wrenches decorated most of the wall space. Behind his desk hung a bulletin board with outdated messages pinned in random fashion.

"What can I do for you two?" Bill asked.

"Did you hear about the events at the airport last night?"

He looked away from them, taking a hold of his Big Gulp soda and giving it a good sip before answering. "Nope. You talking about the big airport or the local one nearby?"

"The one down the road. What is it, two tenths of a mile away, right?"

"I suppose," he admitted. He seemed in no hurry to get on with the conversation, though Tom could tell he was nervous by the way he drummed his fingers on the tabletop. After the silence stretched a bit longer, Melton prompted, "You were saying a disturbance?"

"Yeah. We busted a plane full of heroin that landed about three thirty this morning."

"Really? Hmm. I suppose that's interesting. Don't see how it concerns me, though."

Tom leaned forward, putting both his hands on the chief's desk. "You don't, huh? A plane full of drugs lands at an airport less than a quarter-mile away, a place where your fire trucks frequently go to do drills, and it doesn't interest you?"

Bill looked at him blankly. "Can't say that it does, Mr. Hill. Can't say that it does."

Back in their car, Tom said to Ester, "He's lying."

"Obviously," she agreed. "Let's go over and check out the airport again."

They drove back to the airport and onto the runway.

"Look here," Ester said. "There's a big drainage grate right next to where both planes parked."

Tom went up and looked down through the grate. "Yeah. This area's prone to flooding. I think I remember there was a bond issue a few years ago regarding putting in new drainage pipes."

"Do you remember this morning when we made the bust, some sort of noise?"

Tom thought back. "Yeah, some sort of clang. I thought it was the Cessna's luggage door coming open."

Ester bent down and struggled to lift the grate a few inches. It made a loud clang when she dropped it. The two officers stared at each other.

Tom lifted the grate open and found a ladder just inside. He climbed down and looked around with his flashlight.

"It's big enough to stand in," he called up to Ester. Climbing back out he said, "Let's head back to the office and find out where it goes."

Just before five o'clock, Stan Hamburg of the DEA came in. "You did a good job, Tom. At least we've plugged up this hole."

"At least?"

"Well, we'd like to get the main guy. You have any information from your mole?"

Tom nodded. "As a matter of fact, he gave me the name and location of the big boss. It's Don Carlos Cantrell. Ever heard of him?"

Stan smiled. "That's great news – we've heard rumors that he might be involved. Now that we have an eyewitness, maybe we can get permission from the State Department to take a task force down there and capture him for extradition. Since it's your man down there, you might want to come down and help make the bust."

"I'd love to!"

As soon as he'd left, Tom called Ester to ask her if she would like to go to dinner. She agreed, but said it had to be some place nicer than

McGill's. She suggested the Aria, and they agreed to meet there at seven.

Tom greeted his lovely date at the front entrance of the restaurant. "I've reserved a table way in the back, dark and quiet, so we could have some privacy."

"Oh? That sounds intriguing. Do you have something special planned that needs a dark location?" she teased.

During their pleasant meal, Tom told her about Stan's invitation to take part in the Colombian raid. She became very excited, telling him she'd make sure she was included on the trip. They dined and talked for two hours.

"It's only nine," Tom commented. "How about coming by my place for a drink?"

She looked at him coyly. "I don't know. Neither one of us got much sleep last night. If I come over, am I going to be crashing on your couch again?"

Tom grinned. "Maybe. Maybe not. Let's see what happens."

Once back at his townhouse, Tom brought beers for himself and Ester. He turned on some soft music and they cuddled up next to each other on the couch. They talked for a bit, and then he stood, pulling her up by the hand, and then close to his chest for some slow dancing.

On the second dance, he led her out of the living room and into his bedroom. There they kissed, undressed, and made slow sweet love.

The next morning at the office, he checked his message machine, eager to hear Manuel's daily report. To his concern, there wasn't any word from his friend. Something had gone wrong.

He began working on the paperwork about the drug bust, as well as reading the reports from the other officers. An hour later Ester rushed into Tom's office with a big smile on her face.

"I got the utility schematics from the planning commission," she reported. "Two years ago, six-foot diameter drainage pipes were laid. The plan was to connect them to the already existing storm drainage lines and run them out to the river. However, the only part of the project that was ever completed was the section running from that old airport, past the fire station, and dumping into the river behind them!"

Tom's face broke into a smile, too. "Well, well, well. So now we know how the drugs were unloaded."

"Right," Ester agreed. "The plane stops on the runway next to the grate. A few firemen climb out of the tunnel, unload the drugs into the tunnel, and cart it away. The whole project could easily be accomplished in fifteen minutes without the pilot or the passengers having any idea it was happening. The passengers really are innocent. They're not told anything about what's going on and are just being used as part of the cover story."

"And the DC-9 was a red herring too! Man, that fire chief must have had some great political pull to get those pipes installed." His smile disappeared.

"What's wrong?" Ester asked.

"I'm worried about Manuel Gomez. He's been very reliable about calling in his daily report, but today he didn't make one. He told me yesterday that he had been called in for a big meeting at the boss's house. I wonder if they suspect him as being the leak for the big bust we made."

Ester put her hand on his arm. "We'll go down there and get him out. Don't worry."

# CHAPTER SEVEN

The next day, Thursday, the task force leaders met for a planning session, led by Stan Hamburg.

"I've secured permission from the State Department and Homeland Security to lead a raid into Bogota, arrest Don Cantrell, and bring him back to the states. We'll take a four-man swat team down, led by Marty Wilson here. In addition, Tom Hill will represent the Atlanta police department because they have an undercover agent there we hope to extract. Ester Allison will go as the FBI representative."

"What do we know about Cantrell's hacienda?" Wilson asked.

"Unfortunately, not much." Stan passed out photographs that showed a satellite photo of the area. "As you can see, it's a walled complex with a guarded gate. We know nothing about any other defenses, either personnel or electronics. It sure would be helpful if we knew someone who'd been inside."

Tom spoke up. "I just might have a lead there. I've …" he hesitated and glanced at Ester. "I mean, we believe that a local fire chief by the name of Bill Melton is deeply involved. It's possible he's actually been down there and seen the hacienda. I suggest we bring him in for questioning."

Tom sent two of his officers to the fire station, and within an hour they came back with Melton, dressed nicely in shiny handcuffs. They took him to an interrogation room where he was locked to a chair, with Tom on the other side of the table and one of the officers standing guard by the door. Police chief Daniel Snife, SWAT team leader Marty Wilson, FBI agent Ester Allison, and DEA Stan Hamburg watched from behind one-way glass.

Tom turned on the tape recorder. "You're been read your rights, correct?"

Melton nodded. "Yeah, and I have nothing to say until I talk to my lawyer."

"So far we haven't charged you with anything," Tom responded. "Just have a listen first, and then if you still want a lawyer, we'll take you to a cell and wait on him. Is that okay?"

The fire chief shrugged. "I'll listen."

"We subpoenaed your bank account records. It seems you've built up quite a nest egg in the past two years. Three quarters of a million dollars!"

Melton shrugged. "That doesn't prove anything."

"It does when it comes from illegal activity, specifically drug running. We know about the special tunnel you had built using city funds running between the airport and the fire station. We know about the drug smuggling you've been doing with it for the past two years. We have enough evidence to put you away for the rest of your life."

Melton picked up the glass of water that had been provided for him and took a swallow. "So far it sounds like I should have a lawyer before I say anything."

Tom reviewed his notes. "Maybe so. We can do it the hard way if you want. On the other hand, I've been authorized by both the city prosecutor and the FBI to offer you a deal."

Melton perked up. "Yeah? What kind of deal?"

"First off, let me list the charges you're currently facing. Ten years in the state penitentiary for swindling the city out of $500,000 for unneeded drainage ditches. Five additional years on the same issue for the felony offense of abusing your office. The biggest crime, of course, is the drug smuggling charge, which carries a twenty-five-year sentence."

Tom took a minute to let that sink in. He could see sweat forming on Melton's brow.

"Then there's the matter of someone shooting me in the shoulder last month. We haven't done ballistics yet, but we know you keep a gun in your office. Shooting a police officer might add another twenty-years to your sentence. You're forty-two years old now. With all these charges, even for good behavior, you'd be in prison for the rest of your life. And, of course, you would lose your home and the $750,000 in your bank account."

The two men stared at each other for a few minutes. Finally, Melton said, "You said something about a deal?"

"Yes, but it depends on one fact. Have you ever been in Don Carlos Cantrell's hacienda?"

Melton asked if he could smoke, and when Tom nodded, the fire chief took out a cigarette, lit it, and smoked it down to ashes.

"You know," Melton said, "if I admit to being in Cantrell's hacienda, I'm pretty much admitting to everything. If I say 'yes,' what are the terms of the deal?"

"A very generous one. We're willing to drop the city charges against you completely, providing you reimburse the $500,000 cost of the drainage pipes. You'd still have a quarter of a million dollars in the bank and keep your home. More importantly, we're willing to reduce the drug smuggling charges to the minor offense of distribution, which would carry only a one-year prison term."

"Let's say I was interested. What would you want in exchange?"

"Information. Most importantly, we need a sketch of Cantrell's hacienda, its layout, the guards, and anything you can tell us about its security system. Second, we need names. We want a list of all the local and international people involved in the drug dealing, and your willingness to testify to their participation. Also, and incidentally, I'm wondering if you have any information about one of my officers who was undercover and now has disappeared."

Melton smoked a second cigarette as he considered the offer. "I hate to turn on my friends, but, hey, I guess they all knew what they were getting into. However, squealing on a drug lord would mean my life ain't gonna be worth a plugged nickel. He'll send hitmen up and kill me. I'd have to be put into a witness protection program, with a new name and new job in a new city."

Tom drummed his fingers on the table. "I'd have to clear that with the FBI, but I would think that's doable. Can you draw us a map of the hacienda?"

"Yeah. Cantrell flew me down once for a personal meeting. Turns out he likes to meet the people he's working with, see if he feels he can trust them."

"Really? You can give us a floor plan?"

"I could sketch it out for you, as well as provide some information about their security system. Not that I know a lot after only one visit, but I kept my eyes open."

"What about my undercover officer?"

Melton shrugged. "I don't know anything about your undercover cop. How would I? But I'll tell you this, those guys play rough. If they think your fellow was a spy, he's probably already dead."

"You understand that if you lie to us about anything, even lies of omission, all deals will be off?"

Melton chuckled. "Fellow, you got me over a barrel. I'm willing to 'fess up on the terms you've listed."

Over the next few hours, Melton made a list of all the local people he'd worked with, both the firemen who helped with the drug unloading and transport as well as his contacts in Colombia and here for distribution. He made a reasonable sketch of the hacienda, indicating some of the security features he'd noticed. Afterwards he was put in solitary confinement to prevent him from notifying anyone.

Marty Wilson examined Melton's sketch carefully.

"We need to do this quickly," Wilson stated. "I'll get my SWAT team together and we'll leave tomorrow night."

"How about Ester and I leave tonight, you know, as an advance team?" Tom suggested. "She and I could pretend we're on our honeymoon and scout out the area."

Wilson scowled. "I don't think it's a good idea. You might be identified, tipping them off to our arrival. And what if you're captured?"

Ester said, "I'm willing to go. There's a plane leaving for Bogota from the Atlanta airport in two hours."

Wilson looked at Hamburg who nodded. "Allison is an excellent agent: brave, confident, an excellent marksman, and speaks Spanish."

"Okay, then," Wilson said. "Go ahead. We'll arrange for your tickets and a hotel room which we'll rent for a week as part of the honeymoon cover story. The rest of the squad will meet you there in two days." He put a hand on Tom's shoulder. "Listen, buddy. Be careful!"

# CHAPTER EIGHT

In three hours, Tom and Ester were sitting next to each other, business class, on a Delta non-stop flight when the stewardess brought their dinner tray. Though not technically on duty, they turned down her offer of alcohol.

"Are you scared?" Ester asked him.

He rubbed his chin considering his answer. "Hadn't thought about it. I guess not. I mean, it's a police case just like any other. We're going down to arrest a bad guy. I am a bit worried about my friend Manuel though."

"I don't mean to cast bad karma, but, well, you haven't heard from him in three days now. These are dangerous men. If they found out he was an undercover agent ..."

"I know what you're trying to say," Tom admitted, "but I have a feeling he's still alive. In any case, we'll find out soon enough."

Tom watched her eat. "You know," he said, "At first I didn't think that we would make a very good team, let alone a romantic couple."

She put down her fork and looked him in the eyes. "Tell me why not, in both cases."

"When we first met I thought you were a bossy braggart and didn't respect my abilities."

"That's so funny," she said with a laugh. "I thought the same thing about you! I guess we're both used to coming on strong, huh? Okay, now tell me about the romantic couple part."

He gave her a wry smile. "I've never been very talented at dating. I guess that's the coming on strong part again, but actually, I'm so much of what they call a Southern Gentleman, I'm shy around women."

"And now?" she asked, a twinkle in her eye.

He coughed. "I ... I think that I've fallen in love with you."

She laid her hand on his. "I've grown fond of you, also, but we have to leave our emotions behind until this trip is over. It's going to be dangerous."

"Right. Okay, just remember. When we get back to the States, we need to have a serious discussion about where we're going."

She gave him a wink, and then put her headrest back and closed her eyes for a quick nap.

They were met coming out of customs by four Columbian soldiers.

"What's up?" Tom asked.

The officer with stripes on his shoulder stepped up. His English was excellent, with only a slight Spanish accent. "Welcome to Colombia, Mr. and Mrs. Hill. My name is Sergeant Victor Rodriguez, security officer. The immigration authority just informed us that we have an honored visitor from the United States, a police officer from Atlanta."

"Yes, that's right. But my visit isn't about police business. My wife and I have just gotten married and are here as tourists on our honeymoon."

"Congratulations. We're here to offer professional courtesy. Colombia can be a dangerous place, especially for American police officers. Please accept my offer as escort to you and your lovely bride to your hotel. I'd also like to post a twenty-four-hour guard – again, solely as a courtesy."

Tom glanced at Ester, who shook her head. Turning back to the agent, Tom said, "I appreciate your concern. No offense, but we'd really prefer to keep this visit very low key. We'll take a taxi to our hotel without the police escort."

The officer raised one eyebrow. "Really?" He had a short discussion in rapid Spanish with his men. One of the other officers looked alarmed, and a third bemused. Turning back to Tom, the sergeant gave a slight bow. "Good luck, Mr. and Mrs. Hill. If you need anything, here's my card."

Tom placed the card in his wallet and, once out on the street, hailed a taxi. Ester gave the address in Spanish and in short order they were checked into their luxury suite. They'd just finished unpacking when a knock came to the hotel door. Tom opened it to find a steward pushing a cart with champagne and fruit.

"A gift for the newlyweds, compliments of the hotel manager."

"Oh darling," he called. Ester came out of the bedroom, her eyes wide. "Look what the hotel manager sent up! Let's have a toast to our happy marriage."

The steward opened the bottle and poured two glasses. Tom took one and handed the other to Ester.

"A toast then. In love forever."

She responded, "And a family of chubby little ones."

The steward bowed and left them. As soon as the door closed behind him, the couple emptied the untasted glasses and the rest of the bottle into the sink.

"I wonder if they were testing us to see if we'd drink," Ester mused. "Maybe that little pantomime will prove to them we're only honeymooners."

That evening they had a lovely dinner at the hotel's restaurant with a pair of cellists serenading them. They enjoyed the king size bed that evening, and the next morning the hotel's bountiful breakfast buffet.

"The SWAT team will be arriving about six. What do you think we should do with our day?" Ester asked.

"Let's drive around to a few of the tourist spots, making sure we're not being followed. Then, maybe we could drive out towards Cantrell's hacienda, sort of get a lay of the land."

Tom rented a car at the hotel desk, and within an hour they headed out. They took a two-hour tour of the Museo Boteo followed by a leisurely lunch in an outdoor café. The whole time they kept their eyes peeled for danger. However, as near as they could tell, no one was following them. In the afternoon they drove out towards the Hacienda, a twenty-mile trip. They got within a quarter-mile before deciding to turn back. "Can't risk being seen next to his house yet," Tom insisted.

Once back at their hotel, they studied the drawings of the drug lord's house. At six o'clock Wilson came by their hotel.

"We're all set for the raid," he told them. "You learn anything?"

"We drove out to his house," Tom reported. "It's pretty straight forward for the first eighteen miles, four-lane highway. But the last two take you up into the hills. A convoy going that way would be easily spotted. It's about a forty-five-minute drive in all."

"Got it. We should be able to fit all our men into two cars, with yours that makes three, and all arrive separately." On a satellite map, he pointed to a fast-food parking lot a block away from the hacienda. "We'll meet here at 2000."

"Can we make it 8:16?" Tom asked.

Wilson looked puzzled. "Why the odd time?"

"Just humor me."

At 7:33 Tom drove he and Ester onto the busy streets. It was past rush hour and their drive went well, bringing them to the meet-up spot two-minutes early.

A SWAT member accompanied a specialist in security for the first approach. In five minutes, they called back and reported they'd killed the guard at the gatehouse and successfully turned off all the electronic security. The rest of the team followed and gathered at the front door. Just inside they found two guards, both of whom were promptly eliminated by use of crossbows to maintain silence. Tom and Ester followed the team as they made their way through the house to the main sitting room where they hoped to find Don Carlos Cantrell.

In a minute they were standing at its threshold where Ester listened with her ear against the closed door. After a minute she turned to the group and whispered, "I only hear two voices, Don Carlos and another man. It sounds like they're questioning a detainee, taking turns hitting him and demanding that he reveal his secrets."

"On three," Wilson whispered. He counted and the SWAT team and two officers crashed into the room. There they found a bodyguard with a loaded gun. His moment of surprise at seeing them gave Ester the opportunity to place a bullet through the smack middle of the man's forehead. Don Carlos and another man raised their hands and surrendered. A man with bloody face seemed to be unconscious, slumped in a chair. Tom shouted in relief. The detainee was Manuel Gomez.

Tom untied him as Ester brought Manuel a glass of water. After he'd downed it, he gave a sarcastic grin. "Thanks for rescuing me, Tom. Just wondering what the hell took you so long? I was getting hungry."

Wilson with two members of the SWAT team rushed Cantrell off to the airport and from there onto a private jet that took off for the states. Tom took out the card he'd been given at the airport and called Officer Rodriguez. The Colombian officer wouldn't at first believe it when Tom gave him the report that Cantrell was on his way to the United States.

"You … you're not only still alive but you took down the Cantrell Cartel! Mr. Hill, I must admit, I'm astounded! Congratulations. My men will be there in one hour."

The other SWAT member stayed with Ester, Manuel, and Tom to search and secure the house until the Colombian police could arrive. Ester worked on bandaging up Manuel, which included making a splint and sling for his broken right arm.

"That man's tough," she told Tom. "I had to set the arm when I applied a splint, and he didn't even whimper. Grimace maybe, but not whimper."

Manuel led them to a room that contained about 50 pounds of unwrapped heroin and another one that had a table laden with bundles of $100 bills, each in packages of 100, so $10,000 a pop. Tom whistled. There had to be a couple of million dollars laying on that table. When Manuel and Ester left the room, Tom slipped ten of the packages in his pocket.

He accompanied Manuel back upstairs where, using the first aid kit that they had brought, Ester placed stitches in several locations on Manuel's face and shoulder. She patted him on the arm. "There you go. This should hold you until we get you back to the States."

"Wow," Tom said. "You can do everything. Shoot like a marksman, karate chop perverts, speak fluent Spanish, and now put in stitches."

"And I make a mean lasagna too ... and with just enough salt."

"Say, would you mind checking on the SWAT agent?" he asked. As soon as she had left, Tom unwrapped the swathing around Manuel's arm, and rewrapped it with the money from his pocket inside.

"What are you doing?" Manuel asked.

"Just adding extra support to the splint," he replied. "Now when we get home, you have your wife unwrap this and rewrap it BEFORE you go the doctor. That's an order."

Manuel saluted. "Okay, Chief. Whatever you say."

They heard a clamor in the entry and, stepping into the hall, they discovered that the Colombian police had arrived.

Officer Rodriguez strode up and shook Tom's hand. "You have done an excellent job. My most sincere congratulations and deep thanks."

"You're welcome. There're two rooms just down those stairs, one with heroin and a second with stacks of money."

The SWAT team member rode with Tom, Ester, and Manuel back to the airport where a small jet waited for them. In no time, they'd taken off on their way back to the USA.

"So what now?" Tom asked her.

Ester gave him a wink. "I guess the job is done. Perhaps it's time for me to get back to my home in D.C."

He sat quietly for a minute, and then took her hand. "Do you have to go back right away? Maybe you could stay in Atlanta for another couple of weeks. You know, maybe some R & R?"

She cocked her head. "I don't think the government will keep paying for my hotel if I'm just on vacation. I hear that Alice has an extra bedroom in her house."

Tom took hold of her other hand. "I don't have an extra room, but I do have a nice comfortable bed. I mean, if you don't mind sharing."

She leaned forward and kissed him. "Okay. I think I can share."

# CHAPTER NINE

Back in the States, safe and sound, Ester moved into Tom's townhouse, and over the next few days found they enjoyed living together. They had a few clashes, Tom's obsessive-compulsive neatness tendency drove her crazy every time she set down her coffee cup and he cleaned it before she had finished. But mostly they worked out their differences.

After five days, Tom decided he would ask Ester to marry him. He picked out a lovely engagement ring with two pearls held together by handcuffs. He called Manuel and suggested he and wife join Ester and him at the Aria for dinner that night where he could present her with the ring and pop the question.

The four of them enjoyed a delicious meal. Tom, Manuel, and Maria all ordered the prime rib, baked potato, and carrots. Ester requested the vegetable lasagna.

After they started eating, Tom asked her if it needed salt.

She shook her head. "Not at this restaurant, Mr. Impulsive."

"Speaking of impulsive, I have something to ask you." He reached into his pocket and brought out the box with the engagement ring he'd purchased. "Ester, I've never felt this way about a woman before. I love you with my whole heart. Would you please consider ... will you be my ..."

He was interrupted by a clatter from the front of the restaurant. Three men came striding to their table, one flashing a badge with an FBI shield.

"Tom Hill?" he asked.

He nodded.

"You're under arrest for drug tracking."

Tom stood. "What are you talking about?"

The agent pointed at Manuel. "Did you or did you not smuggle in $100,000 of drug money on the body of Officer Gomez coming back from Colombia?"

Tom turned to his friend, who had a fresh cast on his arm. "Manuel? That money was for you and your wife."

Manuel opened his palms. "Sorry Chief. As soon as Maria unwrapped the swathing and we found the money, we called the FBI right away. We told them you had used me for smuggling it in."

Tom stood with head hung as the officer read him his rights and handcuffed him. The other three watched from their table as Tom was led out the door.

"You know," Ester said, "I'm not so sure I really loved him. I mean, he's handsome, neat, brave, tough, and has good manners. But he was a bit of a braggart, you know?"

The waiter came to the table very apologetically. "I hope your evening hasn't been ruined. Is there anything I can do?"

Manuel nodded. "Yes, please. We'll have two Crème Brûlées and one tiramisu, along with three large brandies."

"Yes, sir, right away, sir," the waiter said, and scurried off.


END

www.ingramcontent.com/pod-product-compliance
Lightning Source LLC
Chambersburg PA
CBHW022048170626
46808CB00003B/1404